·ARION·
·and·the·
·DOLPHIN·

To the wild Irish dolphin, "Fungie" — V.S.
To David — J.R.

This book is based on the libretto written by
Vikram Seth for the opera *Arion and the Dolphin,*
composed by Alec Roth. The opera was commissioned by
the Baylis Program of the English National Opera and was
first performed in Plymouth in June 1994.

Text copyright © 1994 by Vikram Seth
Illustrations copyright © 1994 by Jane Ray
All rights reserved.
CIP Data is available.
Published in the United States 1995 by
Dutton Children's Books,
a division of Penguin Books USA Inc.
375 Hudson Street
New York, New York 10014
Originally published in Great Britain
1994 by Orion Children's Books, London
Typography by Carolyn Boschi
Printed in Italy
First American Edition
1 3 5 7 9 10 8 6 4 2
ISBN 0-525-45384-9

·ARION· ·and·the· ·DOLPHIN·

·by·Vikram·Seth·
·illustrated·by·
·Jane·Ray·

DUTTON CHILDREN'S BOOKS · NEW YORK

One starry night in Corinth, the young musician Arion sat talking with his lord and master, the tyrant Periander.

"A music competition in Sicily?" said Periander. "I won't have it!"

"Sir, let me go," pleaded Arion. "If I win, my songs will spread your fame."

"If you win! But if you don't win, you die! Oh, I suppose you can go, as long as you come back," said Periander.

"I'll win, and I promise to return," said Arion.

"One last song, then," said Periander, and Arion sang.

Bright stars, guide me to fame
By land, by sea—
So that my form and name
May rest among you in the sky.
And you, dark restless sea,
Be gentle on my way
From Greece to Sicily.

Arion set sail for Sicily. He talked to the ship's captain, who was glad to have him for company, and listened to the sailors singing as they worked.

Our decks are scrubbed and clean,
    sang the sailors,
Our ropes run strong and free.
    Fair winds, fill out our sails,
    Bring us no gusts or gales,
    Keep us from sharks and whales
From Greece to Sicily.

"Arion! Let's hear you sing!" shouted
one of the sailors, and Arion joined in.

Dark, restless sea,
Blue, green, black, gray,
Be gentle on my way
From Greece to Sicily.
   May no storm shake the sky,
   Or seagulls wheel and cry,
   But dolphins dip and fly
Beside my ship and me.

Well, with a voice like that, I'm not surprised Periander didn't want to let you go," said the captain. "Look, there's Sicily ahead of us! And here's my parting gift to you. I've enjoyed having you on board."

Arion, keep this shell.
It is a gift from me,
So guard it well.
It will make music in your ear
Whenever you choose to hear
The ocean's surge, its rustling harmony.
Arion, keep this shell.
Be well, be well.

Crowds thronged the harbor to see the ship.
"Who've you got on board?" someone shouted.
   "The winner of your competition, for one!" said
the captain. "Arion will teach you Sicilians how to
sing. Arion, my friend, I must leave you.
I will come back later to take you to Corinth."
   "Let's give him a good time!" said one of the
Sicilians. Arion was pleased. There was plenty of
time to practice before the competition.

But there was no practicing. Arion spent his time feasting and drinking, enjoying his freedom. When at last he stood up to sing, not a sound came out.

"Two false starts is all you get!" said the master of ceremonies.

Despairing, Arion remembered the shell. He put it to his ear and heard the surge of the sea. Softly he began to sing, and as his song grew stronger and sweeter, the Sicilians shouted, "More! More! Arion is the winner!"

Arion accepted his prize of gold. It was
time to leave. He sang one last song:

Dark, restless sea
   Accept my weight once more,
   As gently as before.
   Bear me to Corinth shore
Alive and safe and free.

Back on board ship, Arion slept while the sailors grumbled
to the captain.

"Why should he have that gold? Let's take it!"

"No!" cried the captain. "I will not touch that gold."

"We'll have the gold, or you die! Think of your wife
and children…"

"Then, Arion, *you* must die!" said the captain. "I cannot see my family harmed."

"Spare my life!" cried Arion, waking. "I'll give you all my gold."

"No," said the captain. "When we reach Corinth, you will go back on your promise. You must jump overboard."

"Let me sing one last song," said Arion.

I do not wish to die. I fear to die,
To sink in the reflection of the sky,
At such a fearful depth to be alone,
To merge with shell and coral, slime and stone,
By tentacles caressed, by green fronds curled,
To drown myself in such a silent world.

O world so beautiful, gray olive trees,
Green laurel bushes, tempest-troubled seas,
I shall not see you or the clouds at night
Or the gold stars or sunset's golden light
Or smell the hyacinth or hear the cry
Of eagle or of wolf before I die.

Arion jumped into the
sea. The moon and stars
disappeared. There was
blackness. He was drowning.

Then he was buoyed up, danced and
played with, riding on a dolphin's back.

"I'm not dead, after all!" cried Arion.

"No, not dead," said the dolphin. "You
leaped from the boat. We took you away.
They did not see."

"You saved me," said Arion gratefully.

I'll take you home to Corinth," said the dolphin.
"But first it's time for supper!"
   The dolphins began to catch and pass and
share fish. Arion watched, entranced, while they
played and sang their song.

> Fish gave us a sufficiency
>   Beneath the sea,
>   As you can see.
> We eat with great efficiency
>   Beneath the sea,
>   As you can see.
>
> Our skins are smooth and rubbery,
> Our bulky bodies blubbery.
> We harry herring happily
> And swallow salmon snappily.

   "Let's sing a duet together," said the
dolphin to Arion when they had finished.

So Arion and the dolphin sang together. As they swam toward Corinth, their voices intertwined.

> The days pass one by one,
>   sang Arion.
> I feel my life has just begun—
> And, for the first time, I am having fun!

> In air and water both, our voices part and blend,
> And I, who never sought a friend,
> Have found one in the end.

The dolphin sang:

> I love Arion and would like to be
> Bound to his voice and him eternally.

The days passed, and they swam into the gulf of Corinth,
where fisherfolk crowded around to point and stare.

> *Now, dolphin, you must go,*
> > said Arion.
> *My part is here above, and yours below—*
> *I where the winds, you where the waters flow.*
> *It must be so.*

But the dolphin did not want to leave Arion.

> *With you I will remain,*
> > the dolphin sang,
> *For if we part, we'll never meet again,*
> *And I would die of loneliness and pain.*
> *This I maintain.*

Look, it's Arion riding on a dolphin!" yelled a fisherman. "Tell Periander!"

Periander came hurrying to embrace Arion.

"You won the competition? Where are your prizes? Why are you not with the captain?"

"My lord, my friend the dolphin saved my life," said Arion, and he told his story and how the dolphin wanted to stay with him.

"Absurd!" said Periander. "The captain is a highly trusted man. You're lying! And how do you know the dolphin wants to stay with you? Explain!"

"We spoke, my lord," said Arion.

You spoke? Then command it to speak now so that I may hear dolphin language too," said Periander. "If it speaks, throw it a mackerel. Speak now! Speak!"

But the dolphin was silent.

"Arrest him! He's lying!" roared Periander. The guards led Arion away.

"What about the dolphin, my lord?" asked a fisherman.

"Oh—do what you like with the dolphin!" snapped Periander.

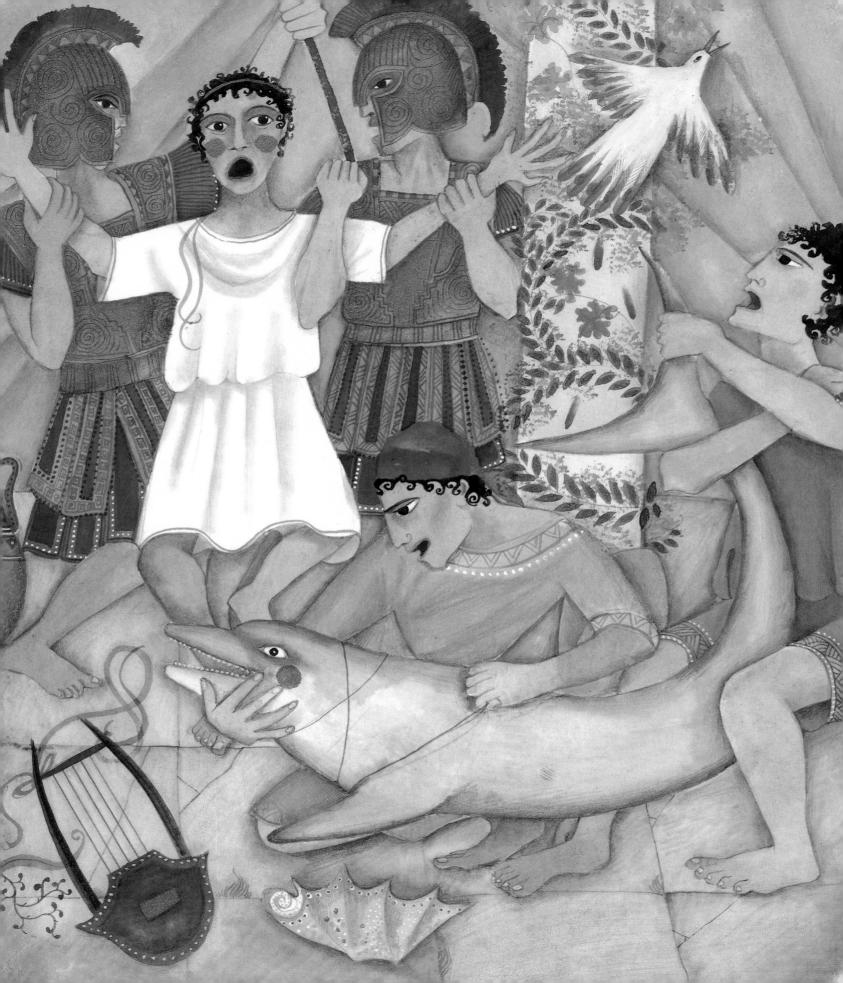

The fisherfolk pushed and poked at the dolphin.
They caged it in a small pool and made people pay
to see it jump for dead fish.

Meanwhile, Arion was locked in a prison cell.
It was not long before a guard came to tell him
the dolphin was dead.

> The dolphin wasted away
> From day to day,
>   said the guard.
> It glutted and it groaned.
> It squeaked, it moaned.
> "Arion...Arion..." all day long
> It seemed to say—a high, pathetic song.
> Into its misery the creature sank.
> Ringed by dead fish, it stank.

Arion's cry of grief made Periander rush into
the cell.

"Forgive me, Arion! I should not have kept you
apart. I will build a tomb for the dolphin, and you
shall go free."

But Arion was not comforted, and as the
dolphin's corpse was brought in, he sang,

Alone am I, and sad that you are dead,
That you are dead, not I—
That you were kind to me, and that led you to die.
When all is done and said,
When all is said and done,
You were my friend, the only one.

The tomb was built, and Arion stayed beside it, grieving. As he lay there, the captain came up from the shore. Periander greeted him politely.

"Welcome home, Captain. A happy voyage, I hope? And where is Arion?"

"He won the contest and the gold," said the captain, "but he chose to leave the ship and return to his birthplace."

"Why do you look so sad, then, Captain?" said Periander. "Is this true? Swear to me that you do not lie."

The captain hesitated.

Arion stepped forward. He struck a chord on his lyre.

"Arion!" cried the captain. "The gods be praised, you're safe."

But Arion turned away from him.

"Take the man away," said Periander. "I've heard enough.

Put him and all his ruffians to the sword."

"No, let them go, my lord," said Arion. "At least delay their sentence for an hour and let me play to you. Perhaps my words will ease this bitterness."

Periander nodded. "Play, then, and sing. I have caused you pain, but now I will listen."

Arion plucked at his lyre, and sang...

I hear your voice sing out my name by night,
By dawn, by evening light.

Dolphin, it was from your marine caress
That I learned gentleness.

Warm Earth, teach us to nourish, not destroy,
The souls that give us joy.

Bright stars, engrave my dolphin and my lyre
In the night sky with fire.